ORCHARD BOOKS
96 Leonard Street, London EC2A 4XD
Orchard Books Australia
32/45-51 Huntley Street, Alexandria, NSW 2015
ISBN 1 84121 482 5
First published in Great Britain in 1997
First paperback publication in 1998
This edition published in 2003
A CIP catalogue record for this book is available from the British Library.
1 3 5 7 9 10 8 6 4 2 (paperback)
Printed in Great Britain

Frock
Shock

**Ros
Asquith**

ORCHARD BOOKS

One

"These scales are not working!" Claire wailed in despair. "I haven't had a single iced bun for two whole days! And only one choc bar. Er, and not more than six packets of crisps. I'm *never* going to fit into that daft little bridesmaid's dress. It was designed for bubble-brained midgets."

"Jumping up and down probably won't help," said Lizzy kindly. "Of course, as you jump up you'll think you've lost weight...but when you come down, things will look very different."

Claire giggled, "Looks like breaking the scales is the only answer. Then there's no evidence."

The two girls stood gazing gloomily at the scales. Long, thin Lizzy, with her frizz of mad curls that looked like a frightened sheep, was wishing as she so often did that she could have Claire's silky, shiny, smooth hair. Big, round Claire (Eclaire to her friends) with her short stumpy legs was wishing,

as she hardly ever did, that she could have Lizzy's long straight legs. Normally, Eclaire was perfectly happy to be fat, but now, she was miserable.

"Maybe the floor's sloping," suggested Lizzy. "Or how about trying to stand on one foot and breathing in?"

"Breathing in might make me *look* thinner," said Eclaire, "but surely it'll make me *weigh* more. Breathing out will make me weigh less, 'cos I'll have less air in me."

They tried it both ways but it didn't make any difference. Then they moved the scales all round the bathroom, but wherever they put them, and however few toes Eclaire balanced on, and however she breathed (she even tried panting to see if the scales went up and down to the rhythm of her breath) she still weighed a whole lot more than her mother wanted.

"But you're still wearing your watch, and your charm bracelet!" yelled Lizzy with glee.

"Oh, sure," said Eclaire, removing them wearily. "They'll make all the difference. What d'you want me to do? Cut off all my hair? Would that make me light enough?"

"Be fair, Eclaire," said Lizzy. "It's not me that wants you to be thinner. I love you all round and cuddly and bouncy. You *know* I do. It's your mother's stupid idea that you should get thin... oops! Sorry..." Lizzy was embarrassed. She'd lived next door to the Pinns all her life and she hadn't meant to be rude about Mrs Pinn – the last thing she meant to do was to hurt her best friend's feelings.

"Don't worry," said Eclaire, seeing Lizzy blush. "I just don't know what's got into Mum. She's so desperate for me to look nice at horrible cousin Mary's wedding that she's gone off her nut. Trouble is, if I can't starve myself into that pukey dress, I'll have to go to Twigs and Jumbos. I don't think I can stand it."

Twigs and Jumbos was the Mothers and Daughters Keep Fit and Slimming Club that had just opened up the road. It was offering 'Family Discounts' and Eclaire's mother was very keen to take Eclaire along with her, even though Mrs Pinn was thinner than a pipe cleaner.

Lizzy tried to look on the bright side. "Maybe Twigs and Jumbos wouldn't be so bad, just for a week? Might be a bit of a laugh?"

Eclaire gave Lizzy a look that made Lizzy feel like she'd just shot her own granny. "Lizzy," she said, in tones of doom. "It is not a laugh. I thought of that already. I thought I might go in order to tell funny stories about it. So I did go, and I asked to be shown round. And believe me, it wasn't funny."

"What was it like?" Lizzy was fascinated.

"First, they weigh you in front of everyone," gasped Eclaire. "Imagine! Then they give all these poor plump, shy, nervous girls horrible exercises to do and 'Eating Plans' – look, I brought a sample one home."

Twigs and Jumbos, or Skeletons and Ghouls

Eclaire dived out of the bathroom and returned with a flashy looking leaflet covered with pictures of super-slim, ridiculously fit

11

looking young women with huge grins showing rows of teeth like piano keys. Eclaire read aloud, in a mock cheery voice, like one of those people trying to sell you soap powder on TV:

"Twigs and Jumbos – a family business that really cares. Eat your way to health and fitness!

"Monday:

"_Breakfast_: One flakey corn. No milk. Water or black tea or coffee. Artificial sweetener may be added if desired.

"_Lunch_: An egg-cup full of low-fat, lower-taste cottage cheese. You may add a single chive, a diced carrot and a sliver of fruit of your choice. Water or black tea or coffee, as above.

"_Evening Meal_: Choose from a thrilling combination of limp lettuce, soggy celery and old cucumber. How about adding half a slice of tomato for colour? Or you may treat yourself to some watercress! Another speck of cottage cheese, a thimbleful of broiled chicken and half a carrot with all the fat cut off or one walnut may be added! Water or black tea or coffee."

"Yuk!" said Eclaire in disgust. "And it goes on like that all week! 'Eat your way to health and happiness' indeed! More like 'Starve yourself into an early grave!'"

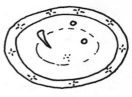

Nourishing meal, Twigs and Jumbos style

"That's terrible! It shouldn't be allowed. Let me see," said Lizzy, making a grab for the leaflet.

"Well, I did make a bit of it up. I don't think there's any fat in carrots... " admitted Eclaire. "But it's nearly as bad as that, honest."

Lizzy thought hard. "Maybe we could kid your Mum you have lost weight? So she won't book Twigs and Jumbos?"

"Well, it might buy a few extra days' grace," said Eclaire. "Will you back me up?"

"Sure," said Lizzy. She felt that a little white lie in a good cause was worth it to save Eclaire from the dreaded clutches of Twigs and Jumbos.

The girls bounced cheerfully downstairs.

"Gosh, Mum!" fibbed Eclaire. "I've lost masses! Isn't that amazing? I don't think I'll have to go to Twigs and Jumbos after all. Shame, I was rather looking forward to it... wasn't I, Lizzy?"

"Er...yes," muttered Lizzy, surprised by this very obvious untruth, but it didn't make any difference.

Eclaire's eagle-eyed mother didn't believe her for a second.

"Marvellous darling," she trilled, "can I just come up and check the scales with you?"

The only vaguely good thing that happened to Eclaire in the next seven minutes was the discovery that she definitely did weigh exactly the same standing on two feet as she had standing on one. Otherwise, all was doom.

"I must have read them wrong," she muttered.

"Yes, they are difficult to see properly in this bright light," said her mother, kindly trying to soften the blow. "But I'm afraid, darling, there's no alternative. We'll just have to go to Twigs and Jumbos for the special seven-session offer. It gets weight off in *no* time. And then you'll be able to fit into that gorgeous dress for Mary's wedding. Just think of the lovely photos!"

"Oh. Yeah. Photos. Hmmm. Great," Eclaire murmured as tall, thin Mrs Pinn went downstairs, patting her pointy, lead-grey hairdo. She always put Lizzy in mind of an HB pencil.

"Marvellous darling, I'll confirm the appointment

for the Ultra-Special Seven-Day Slenderiser course starting next Saturday." Mrs Pinn shouted from the hall. "That's in just eleven days' time. Still rather close to the wedding, of course, which is the Saturday after... Pity I didn't book it before." Mrs Pinn's voice sounded full of regret. Even she had to admit to herself that it was unlikely that her daughter would turn from Jumbo to Twig in a week.

Eclaire was already dreading the thought of cousin Mary's wedding. Lots of girls may dream of being bridesmaids, of floating down aisles in fairy-tale

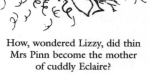

How, wondered Lizzy, did thin Mrs Pinn become the mother of cuddly Eclaire?

frills, clutching little bunches of flowers and smirking prettily. But Eclaire was not one of them.

"As far as I'm concerned," she confided to Lizzy, "weddings are just invented to torture relatives. You have to put on horrible, uncomfortable clothes you wouldn't be seen dead in normally, then stand around for centuries surrounded by dying flowers while some poor old vicar no one's ever met before drones on for hours and then forces everyone to sing – and it's always out of tune."

"Yeah," agreed Lizzy. "Then you have to go off to a revolting 'buffet' where the only food is that really hard white bread that chips your teeth and little sausages that look like dog's mess and the only drink is warm orange juice."

"And you have to listen to uncles you can't remember ever meeting saying how you've grown since they last saw you, which was probably when you were in your pram. I mean, really, who wants to see photos of all that. Especially when you're wearing the Puke-Pink-Dress-of-Horrors... "

The dress Eclaire's mother was trying to get her to wear was not just too small, it was, to Eclaire anyway, breathtakingly, record breakingly, hideous.

"Go on, let me see it," begged Lizzy.

"Only if you solemnly swear not to describe it to a single soul," said Eclaire, "not even to Flash or Owl."

Lizzy agreed and performed the ritual promise that she and Eclaire had been making since they were in Infants School,

I promise on the sun
I promise on the stars
I promise on a bun
And some choccy bars

I swear on the Earth
I swear on the sky
If I break my oath
I'm bound to die.

(They'd added the second bit in Juniors.)

Then Lizzy had to punch herself in the head, cross her hands over her chest and bow three times. It always made her feel a bit creepy (just supposing she did forget and break the promise) but she didn't like to admit it.

Satisfied, Eclaire went into her parents' bedroom and emerged staggering under the weight of a huge box. Layers of tissue paper had to be carefully unwrapped before the dreaded dress could be revealed. It was a pink. It was bound to make whoever wore it, unless they had very dark skin, look pale yellow. It was covered in smocking and frills and flounces and nets. Worst of all, it had a sash *and* a bow.

The Puke-Pink-Dress-of-Horrors.
Was it designed for pantomime?
And why did its wearer have to
carry so many spare tennis racquets?

"Ug," Lizzy had to admit it was disgusting. "It's got frills on its *flounces* – and flounces on its *frills*."

"And you could catch enough fish for the whole school in all that," said Eclaire, gazing sadly at the layers of net.

"And look at that stupid little waist. Even if you starved for a year you'd still look like a hippo trying to pass itself off as a kitten."

Eclaire went a peculiar shade of red.

"I'm sorry, Eclaire, I didn't mean..."

"No. It's funny, it really is," Eclaire collapsed, laughing so hard she nearly choked.

When she had recovered, Lizzy suggested that they might spill something on the dress.

"You know, something like ink, or bleach," she said mischievously.

"No," Eclaire was regretful. "It cost a fortune. Mum would never forgive me. But we've got to have a plan. Maybe I could hire someone to be me for the wedding? There must be a thin look-alike somewhere in the world?"

"Or maybe you could poison the bridegroom? Nothing fatal neccessarily, just something to

19

slow him down for a few years..." suggested Lizzy.

"Till I lose my 'puppy fat'?" asked Eclaire crossly. "Look, I'm fat and happy (I think) and I intend to try to stay that way. On the other hand, poisoning might be an idea for Mary. I never liked her much. She used to call me Fattypuff and sit on my head when I was four..."

"Yeah. You could make her some of your famous Nuclear Nougat." said Lizzy. "Only with real radiation!" she added. "Trouble is," Lizzy went on thoughtfully. "Your mother's obsessed with your being thin like the rest of your strange twig-like relatives. So even if you do scupper the wedding, she'll still need convincing."

This thought made Eclaire feel even worse. "Why, oh *why* do people keep trying to make us different? Your mother's always nagging you about your frizz – I mean, hair. Owl's mother tells her to speak up and stop being shy, even Flash's mum keeps on about 'dressing smartly' 'cos she's so worried about looking as though they haven't got two beans. Lizzy..." Eclaire went on nervously, "be honest, d'you think I should try to get thin? I mean, do you look at me and see a big fat blob? Really?"

"Eclaire! Don't be silly! You know what I think!

You're YOU.
You're YOU.
You're YOU
that's WHO.
And no one else in the world will DO."

Eclaire felt better. "I'm going to eat for England! I'm going to be a master chef and open a chain of restaurants called 'Fatso'! I'm going to make a million from Roly-Polo sweets!"

"But wait a sec," Lizzy interrupted Eclaire. "Your mother wants you to be a twig, but she's pretending she wants you to lose weight just so you can fit into the bridesmaid's dress. So if we can scupper the wedding then she won't have any excuse to nag you, you see."

"Oh, she'll probably find some other vital occasion like her great uncle's nephew's tortoise's barmitzvah," snorted Eclaire, cheering up again. "Still, I like the sound of scuppering the wedding.

You're right, it's worth a try."

"We need a meeting," declared Lizzy solemnly, "of the Fab Four."

Two

Lizzy and Eclaire had set up the Fab Four with their friends Flash and Owl. They had high hopes of secret meetings and exotic mysteries to solve, but so far, things hadn't really turned out like that. But now one of them was in big trouble and it was the Fab Four to the rescue.

Since the problem was urgent, Lizzy and Eclaire went straight round to Owl's house.

"Owl," they shouted, as tiny Owl opened the door. "Mega-problem. Urgent meeting required!"

"B-but I w-was j-just..." stammered Owl.

Owl had been balancing on top of her tiny platform bed putting up a poster of Lord Nikolai, who was not a rock star or a footballer but a famous Shakespearian actor. Lord Nikolai would have to wait, which he did, hanging upside down and gazing, with his large actor's eyes, into Owl's goldfish bowl.

"No excuses," said Lizzy, and poured out the story.

"W-w-well Flash is sure to have some ideas," whispered Owl. "Let's ring her and ask her to come round."

The girls rushed to the phone.

"Can't come," croaked Flash, "got the lurgi."

The lurgi had whipped round school like a whirlwind all term, laying low pupils with a mix of sore throat, lumpy neck and high fever. Flash, being the sportiest, fittest girl in town, was the last to get it.

"Flash with the lurgi," said Lizzy. "Wonder of wonders. We'll just have to have a meeting of the Fab Three, instead."

"No, that's n-n-not fair," whispered Owl. "Flash should be included. W-we could go over there."

Owl, as well as being incredibly small, was extremely timid. If Owl said "Boo" to a goose (an unlikely event in the first place), it would honk rudely. Mice, voles and other shy creatures seemed like circus performers next to her. Also, Lizzy and Eclaire knew that Owl didn't like going to Flash's flat, as it was on the top storey of a thirteen-floor tower block and Owl was very superstitious.

Actually, Lizzy and Eclaire were quite superstitious themselves, although they always pretended they went round ladders, avoided cracks in the pavement and skipped thirteen when counting just for a laugh. Still, they were impressed that little Owl was so determined to include Flash.

"You're right Owl. Of course we should go," said Lizzy. "Flash would feel really left out. Anyway, we've all had the lurgi, so we can't catch it."

"Huh. Wish I could," muttered Eclaire. "Then I could skive off the wedding."

Owl's superstitions deepened when they discovered the tower block lift was out of order.

"Full of wee anyway," said Lizzy, wrinkling her nose.

But as they climbed the stairs, which were covered in graffiti and old mattresses, they all thought, not for the first time, how lucky they were not to live here.

But Flash's flat, which she shared with her mother and the not-very-nice lodger, Snake, was a haven of cosiness. Flash's mum grew geraniums everywhere – inside and out – and Flash was lying on her camp bed in the living room (Snake had the

YOU &
YOUR PONY

TISSUES

only other bedroom apart from her mum's), guzzling a huge box of chocolates and reading *You and Your Pony*. Flash was horse-mad. She spent every spare minute mucking out at the local riding school in exchange for free rides. But she knew that even in stories, kids never got to keep ponies in the window boxes of tower blocks, so she made up for it by having model horses everywhere. Little ponies of all shapes and sizes, made of felt, fur, china, wood, rubber and glass, were dotted round the room, peering through the geraniums, and a vast poster of a palomino stallion was stuck above the cranky old gas fire.

"Mum's really spoiling me," she croaked as the other three crowded into the little room and flopped onto the bed. "Since she got her job back, she's bought me something nearly every day. Today I got chocs *and* this." She showed them a tiny silver horse on a chain. "I'm gonna wear it for ever."

Flash's mother was a school dinner lady and everyone knew that even with the rent from the slimy Snake, things were very tight in the Fox household. Which is why, when Flash offered them orange juice, they all said they'd prefer water, thanks very much. Mrs Fox bought in a big jug full of iced water with some mint leaves in it and six biscuits.

"None for you, darling, they'll hurt your throat," she told Flash. "Have fun, girls," Mrs Fox winked. It was thanks to the Fab Four that she'd got her job back, she guessed they had some plot to hatch.

Lizzy brushed back her frizzy hair and cleared her throat.

"There is a big crisis in the life of one of our fabulous members, Eclaire. In order to solve this pressing problem I declare this meeting of the Fab Four open."

And they all chanted:

"All for one and one for all
Fatty, skinny, short and tall
Frizzy, Flash, Owl and Eclaire
Stick together, foul or fair.

Four for one and one for four
Funny, clever, rich and poor
Frizzy, Flash, Eclaire and Owl
Stick together, fair or foul"

"Twigs and Jumbos!" squawked Flash in a frenzy, the minute she'd heard the story. "Pull the other one! Do you know what those stupid dieting courses *cost*?"

"It's a special offer," muttered Eclaire, embarrassed.

"Yeah, but they're such a rip-off. And even if you get thin, you get fat again a week later."

"Flash," said Lizzy quietly, "we know that. We're trying to get Eclaire *out* of Twigs and Jumbos, not *in* to it."

"I should hope so too," sulked Flash.

"So is it poisoning or a look-alike?" asked Lizzy, thoughtfully.

"What?" yelled Flash and Owl staring at her.

"Poisoning or a look-alike," Lizzy said firmly. "That's all we've come up with so far. Either we get someone who looks like Eclaire, only thin, or we poison the bride, or we poison the groom."

"Great idea," snorted Flash. "You find a look-alike. How? By advertising? And then you get her to live with Mr and Mrs Pinn for a week until the wedding. And what do you pay her? And where do you hide Eclaire?" Flash, whose throat was cracking under the strain of this speech, gulped a tumbler of water and sank back on her pillow, gasping. "I like poisoning though, neat."

"V-very d-dramatic," whispered Owl. "Makes me think of Shakespeare. W-we could get something from the chemist's and pour it into the groom's ear while he's sleeping."

"Yeah. Ear drops. Get real, Owl, we have to think of something that will work and won't get us put in prison. Anyway, I think I've experimented enough with potions recently," said Lizzy, taking command. She didn't usually get the chance when Flash was well.

"Well," said Eclaire "we don't have to *kill* either of them. We could just give them something to make them feel really really ill..."

"What about a break-in?" croaked Flash. "We could stage a burglary and steal the bridesmaid's dress."

"Oh, brilliant." Lizzy was heavily sarcastic. "I can just see the Pinns believing that. 'Good heavens!' they'd say 'Look! A burglar's been, and ignored the video, ignored the TV, ignored the computer and just taken the bridesmaid's dress. How strange.'"

"W-well," giggled Owl. "We could s-steal everything."

There was a stunned silence.

"And – and return it, of course," said Owl hastily.

"Sure," said Lizzy. "Or just leave a note saying 'We're from a poor family and we need a dress for our poor little daughter...'"

"I know," Eclaire had a brainwave. You could almost see the light bulb flashing above her head as she spoke. "We could get them to call the wedding off."

"Who?" chorused Owl, Flash and Lizzy.

"The happy couple of course," said Eclaire. "Let's make them fall out. You know, fall out of love. Have a big row and call it all off!"

"Hmmmmmmm. Now you're talking," whispered Flash, whose voice was almost as quiet as Owl's.

"But how?" said Lizzy.

"Let's invent another girlfriend," said Eclaire with that light bulb look again.

"Oh, sure. Disguise ourselves as girlfriends of the groom. Pur-leez," scoffed Flash.

"But that could be brilliant," interrupted Lizzy. She suddenly saw herself in scarlet high heels and black net stockings. It would give her a chance to wear a wig, too, and disguise her frizz...

"No. We do it with a *letter*," said Eclaire firmly.

"Or on the phone," whispered Owl.

"Or both..." croaked Flash.

And so the four girls plotted. They knew that Owl was always practising speeches in her bedroom and was brilliant at accents. She would be able to pretend to be another girl as long as she could do it on the telephone. And Lizzy had a knack for copying handwriting.

"So..." went on Eclaire, "If I can get hold of a specimen of Charles's writing, Lizzy can forge a love letter from him to another, complete with a *passionate* reply."

"Who's Charles?" asked Flash, who was not herself, owing to the lurgi.

"The bridegroom, you dodo," said Lizzy.

"Of course. Sorry. Then you'll put both letters into his pocket. But how?" Flash paused.

"Easy. Mary and Charles are coming for supper with my parents on Friday!" Eclaire was really excited now.

"H-hang on a minute," whispered Owl, whose

grasp of plots was very good, because she had read so many plays. "W-why would *b-both* the letters be in his p-pocket? I mean, if he sent a letter to another girl, *she'd* have it, w-wouldn't she?"

This problem flummoxed everyone for some time. But it was Owl who had the solution.

"I know. W-we'll m-make the letter from the g-girlfriend say something about having to return his l-letter for fear her own boyfriend will find out! And...um...th-then go on to say th-that sh-she'll meet him as p-planned to elope!"

"Yeah. And then while they're at your place, Eclaire, you slip the letters into Charles's coat pocket!" said Lizzy. "And then you can easily find a way to make the letters fall out, by barging into him, or dropping his coat or something."

"Yes," said Eclaire rubbing her hands together gleefully. "Meanwhile Owl can ring up, pretending to be Charles's girlfriend! I'll try to put the phone near Mary, then she'll pick it up and hear this other woman asking for Charles. That and the letters will make her so jealous she's bound to break off the engagement!"

"But why would Charles's secret love ring him at your house?" asked Lizzy.

"Um. Obviously, they're – er – so in love, that he gives her every number he's at, in case of an emergency..."

"That might work," said Lizzy, doubtfully.

Everyone was thinking what fun it would be to forge letters and fake phone calls. But the Fab Four were so excited that they had forgotten one vital thing. It was Owl who timidly pointed out their plan's fatal flaw.

"U-um," she ventured nervously, "th-there's j-just one p-problem. How is Eclaire going to get the sample of Ch-Charles's handwriting?"

"Oh no. My brain hurts," groaned Flash. And everyone else's did, too, even Owl's.

"Maybe we'll have to do a break-in after all?" wondered Eclaire.

"What? Climb in your cousin's boyfriend's window? You have to be joking!" scoffed Lizzy.

"No! Wait a minute!" He wrote my mother a note to accept the supper invitation! I remember because she said how nice and polite it was for someone to write a note instead of phoning!"

"Well, so long as you can find the note..." wheezed Flash, who was now looking rather green.

"Poor Flash," said Lizzy. "We've tired you out."

"Rubbish," snorted Flash, with some of her old fire. But they could all tell that she was very tired.

"I declare this meeting closed. All those in favour say 'Meringue'," said Lizzy.

And they all held hands, bellowed "Meringue" at the tops of their voices and chanted:

"All for one and one for all
Fatty, skinny, short and tall
Frizzy, Flash, Owl and Eclaire
Stick together, foul or fair.

Four for one and one for four
Funny, clever, rich and poor
Frizzy, Flash, Eclaire and Owl
Stick together, fair or foul."

Three

"Why don't you put your feet up, Mum? I'll make you a nice cup of tea."

"Goodness Claire," said her mum, surprised. "That would be lovely. No sugar, mind."

"Yes, then you can curl up in front of *The Demon of Suburbia*."

"Lovely. Aren't you going to watch?"

"No. Homework," lied Eclaire.

She was very sorry to miss an episode of *The Demon of Suburbia*. It was the hot new sit-com about a murdering milkman. Still, for Eclaire, duty called.

She crept upstairs to her mother's room to search for the letter. Mrs Pinn was as neat as – well – a pin. She had regular clear-outs, but she usually kept family letters. Eclaire was sure Charles's note would be in the little drawer in her mother's bedside table. But no. Perhaps she'd tucked it in the photo album? Eclaire didn't like looking at the photo album. She couldn't quite say why. Was it because everyone was always smiling, and life wasn't like that? Or was it because – she hated to admit this – there were far more pictures of her thin, handsome older brothers in it than of her? Anyway, a quick flick through the pages revealed no letter. Then it must be in her mother's desk drawer.

Eclaire wished she hadn't looked in her mother's desk drawer. It had about fifty different slimming club leaflets and a big article about fat daughters.

Oh no, she thought, Mum must be really desperate for me to be thin! She must really *hate* the way I look! If Twigs and Jumbos is the best of this lot I dread to think what the others are like.

Suddenly the bedroom door flew open.

"What are you doing in here, Claire?" Her mother sounded unusually cross.

"Oh. Sorry. Um. Looking for sticky tape. School project."

"You know that's in the kitchen table drawer, where it always is. You mustn't go looking through my work things." Mrs Pinn was flustered. "I hope you haven't been reading any of it."

"Of course not. Absolutely not...I just need sticky tape and scissors. Er, and paper clips. And some pipe cleaners. Felt...onions... Got any tin foil?" asked Eclaire wildly.

And in no time she was trapped at the kitchen table, wondering what she could possibly make out of felt, pipe cleaners and tin foil...and wondering *why* she'd said onions! She must be mad. She *could* have just been curled up comfortably on the sofa watching *The Demon of Suburbia.*

She decided she could make a tin foil pyramid and started to wonder:

1) Whether she should use the pyramid for a pretend maths project.

(She munched a chocolate biscuit thoughtfully)
Or

2) whether it would be better for something about the Egyptians, particularly if she used the pipe cleaner to make a Mummy bandaged with felt...

(Her hand reached out for the biscuit packet.)
And

3) What her teacher would say at this unusual display of enthusiasm, since she hadn't been given any homework that evening.

(Two more biscuits bit the dust.)
And

4) How she could possibly raise the subject of Charles's letter with her mum.

(This was a tricky one, another biscuit might help.)
And

5) Whether she actually *was* going a little bit mad? Maybe it was bad to be fat? Certainly, everyone else seemed to think so...

(She looked guiltily at the empty biscuit packet and then scrunched it quickly into the bin.)

Eclaire hardly slept for thinking about the letter. But in the deep, dark middle of the night, she came up with a plan.

"By the way, how was *The Demon of Suburbia*?" she asked innocently at breakfast.

"Oh, brilliant," laughed her mother. "He bumped off two people this time. Apparently viewers all over the country are worried about paying their milk bills now, in case their milkman's The Demon. At least, that's their excuse!"

"Mary and Charles are going to live in suburbia, when they're married, aren't they?" continued Eclaire cheerily, as though the word 'suburbia' had only just put her in mind of the happy couple.

"Hmmm," Mrs Pinn sipped her tea.

"Shame we can't meet him again before the wedding, he seemed nice."

"But they're coming to supper on Friday, Claire. I told you."

"No, surely, you said they couldn't come, didn't you?"

"No. Charles wrote. Such a nice letter," said Mrs Pinn fondly.

"I'm *sure* you said he wrote saying they couldn't make it."

"No, no. Goodness, I didn't say that, did I?" Mrs Pinn began to have doubts.

"Yes, you did," said Eclaire firmly. "You said what a nice letter, how nice of him to write, what a shame they couldn't come."

Mrs Pinn *had* made the first two remarks. She began to feel very unsure of herself.

"Oh dear. Are you sure? I'll have to ring them up."

"I know," said Eclaire, as if she had just thought of the idea, "why not look at the letter again? Maybe he did say they were coming."

"I can't do that, Claire. I binned it."

Mrs Pinn headed for the phone. Eclaire headed for despair. That was it then. No letter, no forgery, no Master Plan. A lifetime – well, a week – of Twigs and Jumbos.

Followed by the Invasion of the Puke-Pink-Dress-of-Horrors. But wait, drifting into Eclaire's thoughts, came another sound...

"Oh, hang on a minute. I did keep it, I think."

This was music to Eclaire's ears. Mrs Pinn rummaged through her bag. "*There* you are. And they *are* coming. Marvellous."

But Eclaire's moment of happiness was brief, because then Mrs Pinn did a really terrible thing. Eclaire watched mesmerised as everything seemed to go into slow motion. As if she were in an action-replay of a cup-final penalty, Mrs Pinn rose from the table, neatly folding the precious note in two and tore it once, twice, three, four times. Then she neatly snapped open the pedal bin and dropped the pieces inside. Then, before Eclaire could speak, Mrs Pinn neatly emptied the tea leaves from the pot all over the torn up letter and, realising the bin was overflowing, neatly plucked out the bin liner, tying it tightly and whisking it out to the dustbins in front of the house.

"Just in time for the dustmen," she said brightly.

Eclaire could hear the clank, clunk of the dustmen's lorry approaching, like a truck of doom.

"Oh. Got to empty my bin," she squeaked, charging out of the room and down the hall as fast as her bendy little legs could carry her.

Alfie Gray, who had been a dustman for forty-two years, had seen some strange sights in the course of his work. He had several times had to fish around a bin in search of engagement rings and once he'd had to rescue a gerbil who had nibbled its way into the family bin liner. But the sight of Eclaire, clad only in her nightie and bunny rabbit slippers, rugby tackling his friend Joe, was one he would never forget.

"She just dived for his legs," Alfie told his wife that night. "Of course, Joe fell, she fell, the dustbin rolled over, they rolled on top of it, it rolled into the gutter, knocking down four other bins, the other bins rolled all down the road...and all that for a few scraps of paper."

"Probably a love letter," said Alfie's wife.

"Nah, she was only a kid. A big kid. But only a kid."

44

By the time Eclaire had picked herself up, consoled
the younger dustman Joe, apologised – and helped
clear up, she hardly had time to think whether it
would be possible to read the soaked and stained
scraps she clutched so tightly. Luckily, her mother
was still sipping tea, blissfully unaware of her

daughter's mad dash. Eclaire slipped upstairs just in time to avoid sarcastic remarks from her two tall, thin, handsome brothers about how she had got egg and tea leaves all over her nightie. She dressed with the speed of light and took the pieces of Charles's note and the roll of sticky tape, to school.

"Don't forget your pyramid, darling," shouted her mother, as she left.

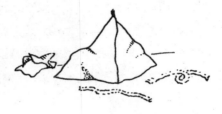

Four

During break time, Eclaire and Lizzy painstakingly stuck the precious letter together. Most of the ink had run and there was a large piece missing. The rest was colourfully stained and smeared with what looked like glue and a fine coating of fluff.

"Is that egg?" asked Lizzy in disgust. "Ugh! I hope that's tomato ketchup... And why on earth is there *toothpaste* on it?"

"Ahaaa," replied Eclaire, speaking in a Mad Scientist voice, "I believe thees bit is definitely stained wiz ze juice of ze fruit of ze rare Pongo-Pongo tree, that only blossoms on ze slopes of extinct volcanoes in ze land of Pong, only once every thousand years."

"And gives off the most terrible *pong*..." laughed Lizzy.

"Oh well, at least we'll be able to read the words 'Dear' and 'Thanks' and 'Charles' – that should be enough to be going on with."

In fact, once they had finished sticking all the bits of paper together, they had plenty to be going on with. What they could read was this:

Dear Mrs. Pi
Thank you so much for
Mary and
lovely
in your
(that glorious hot evening
beautiful romantic
awash with passion
shall never forget the
Roses!
I
ook
eyes
me,
very
love.
ecstatically
little
tired of waiting so long
will be together...
I am thrilled
soon we
bosom
I shall never
I am the luckiest man
forget
alive.
Looking for
ever,
Charles

"Unbelievable!" squealed Lizzy. "It's a gift!" "Mum did say he was romantic," remembered Eclaire. "But what about 'bosom'? What can he really have said? I hope he's not in love with my mum!"

"Don't be daft," said Lizzy, "she'd hardly have torn the letter up, would she?"

Eclaire felt better. In fact, this is what Charles had actually written, although the girls were never to know.

Charles Smith
8 Ponsonby Street
Lovington
LO4 0OH

Dear Mrs. Pinn,

Thank you so much for the kind invitation to supper.

Mary and I would love to come. We both remember the delightful time with you in your lovely home on that glorious hot evening last Summer in your beautiful romantic garden awash with Passion flowers and Roses! And I shall never forget the kind look in your eyes as you gazed on Mary and me, so very much in love. We are ecstatically happy, although a little tired of waiting so long for the wedding! But we are comforted by the knowledge that soon we will be together...

I am thrilled to be welcomed into the bosom of Mary's family in so warm a way. I shall never forget your kindness. I am the luckiest man alive.

Looking forward to seeing you on Friday.

Yours ever,

Charles

They had a lot of fun with Owl that evening, working out what to say. When they'd decided, they rang Flash, who was still in bed, and Eclaire read the letter out to her.

My dear, dear Rose
I am awash with passion!
I shall never forget the
look in your beautiful,
ecstatically lovely ~~bosom~~ eyes
that romantic evening.
I am so very, very ~~very~~ much
in love with you — I am the luckiest
man alive! I am tired of
Mary — and of waiting for
you. I long for the thrill
of your hot bosom. Soon
we will be together forever.
Love, love, love, charles

"That is stunning!" gasped Flash. "But wouldn't he say 'Darling'?"

"Er," Eclaire turned to the others, "Flash says, shouldn't we put 'Darling'?"

"Well... I'd find it difficult to forge words he hasn't actually *used*," snapped Lizzy crossly. Eclaire told Flash. There was a frightening cackling wheeze down the phone, like an old witch with hiccups.

"Flash? Are you all right?"

"Fine," said Flash, gasping for breath. "You don't mean he used *those* words in a thank you note? Read it again."

Eclaire read it again. And again.

Flash was speechless, as much from lurgi as amazement.

"Now," said Eclaire. "You've got to actually write it out, Lizzy. You'll have to copy each word exactly. It's going to be really tough."

"I've th-thought of th-that." said Owl producing a sheet of tracing paper. "See? You can t-trace each w-word separately, then trace th-them all again, j-joined together, then scribble on the b-back with a 2B pencil to transfer them to *this*." She flourished a note pad full of pink paper. "*Then* you'll g-go over them with *this*," she waved a fountain pen.

"Owl, you're a genius," shouted Eclaire, hugging her tiny friend. The largeness of Eclaire and the smallness of Owl resulted in Owl's brief disappearance. She came out of the embrace gasping for air.

"Hang on," said Lizzy. "Charles's original letter to Eclaire's mum was on pale blue paper, with his address printed on top. Maybe we should use the pink paper for Rose's reply!"

"And I could easily forge Charles's printed address on the computer," added Owl.

They had a lot of fun with Rose's letter, too. Flash had begged to be allowed to write it out, since she had been feeling a bit left out. Also, she had very flowery handwriting which seemed suitable.

This is what they wrote from Rose:

My darling, darling Charles,
Your letter filled me
~~with~~ a longing for you which
I am unable to resist. YES!
That evening of passion is ~~ever~~
forever with me! I beg you,
meet me in the arbour on Friday
week at midnight, so that we
can elope as planned before
your wedding night! I am
~~afraid Kevin may find it~~
returning your letter as I am
afraid Kevin may find it and
fly into a jealous fit.
                                    Rose

Meeting in the arbour had been Owl's idea. She said people in Shakespeare's plays often met behind arbours. They were all three very pleased with the letter, and Lizzy and Eclaire said Owl could stay at home to forge Charles's address, while they went round to Flash's so she could copy out the letter from Rose. They took two pink sheets of paper in case she made a mistake the first time.

Flash added a few flourishes of her own and the final result looked like this:

My Dearest, Darlingest, Charles. ♡

Your steamy letter filled me with a torrid longing for your manly form, which I am powerless to resist. Oh yes! That evening of wild passion is forever with me! I beg you, meet me in the harbour on Friday week, at midnight, so that we can elope as planned before your wedding night!

I am returning your beloved, wonderful, adorable, fantastic, gorgeous, scrumptious letter as I am afraid Darth may find it. As you know, if he did, his jealous rage would be so great as to make me fear for our very lives!

A thousand kisses, my darling, on your powerful lips.

All my love,
Your own, your very own,

Rose *❋*
     x
♡

"Oh wow," sighed Lizzy in admiration. "That's just brilliant!"

"Fantastic," agreed Eclaire. "Just one thing, you've put 'harbour' instead of 'arbour'."

"I thought you meant 'harbour'," said Flash. "What, may I ask, is an 'arbour'?"

The other two had been too embarrassed to admit to Owl that they didn't know what an arbour was either, so they just shrugged.

"Oh well," said Lizzy. "There could be a harbour near where Rose lives, couldn't there? And they have to flee the country by boat, perhaps, to escape the rage of Kev – I mean, Darth."

"Hang on," said Flash. "Just a final touch." She slipped off to the bathroom and came back wearing an incredibly large slab of scarlet lipstick and waving a bottle of perfume.

She then covered the letter with kisses and doused it with a spray of *Jardin du Rose.*

"Flash, a finishing touch of pu-u-ure genius!" warbled Lizzy.

So the plan was hatched, and the props were made. Now all it needed was for Eclaire to plant the two letters in Charles's pocket when he came to supper, and for Owl to be stationed in a public phone box with ten twenty-pence pieces, in order to phone up pretending to be Rose...

Five

"No, Claire. Forks on the left, knives on the *right!*
Really! Anyone would think you were a three year
old."

"Why do adults give dinner parties," Eclaire
wondered, "when all it does is make them so bad
tempered?"

"If your father doesn't get back by 7:30, I'll
personally strangle him."

"You've been watching too much telly, Mum,"
giggled Eclaire. But she looked nervously at the
clock. It was 7:15. She patted her pocket for the
hundredth time that day. She felt as if the two
letters, one so pink, one so blue, were burning a
hole in her trousers.

"What's that dreadful smell, dear? Has
something gone off?" Mrs Pinn was peering in the
fridge.

Oh no, thought Eclaire. Flash overdid it with the

Jardin du Rose. She scuttled outside to wave the letter about in the fresh air and get rid of some of the smell.

Mr Pinn arrived with two bottles of wine and a wilting bunch of flowers at 7:50. Mrs Pinn did not strangle him.

"They'll be here in ten minutes," she hissed furiously.

And twelve minutes later, Charles and Mary arrived – looking radiantly happy.

"Let me take your coats," blurted Eclaire, desperate to get a chance to slip the letters into Charles's pocket. But it was a warm spring evening, and he didn't have a coat. Just a jacket, which he was anxious to keep on. Help! She hadn't thought of that.

"Hello *little* cousin," said Mary. "Glad to see you're still into cream buns! Did you and Charles meet last time?"

Eclaire went pink.

"Of course we did," said Charles, rather sweetly. "How could I forget?" He then plonked a huge bouquet of flowers into Mrs Pinn's arms. They were much prettier and fresher than those that Eclaire's dad had bought, so Mrs Pinn took the first bunch out of the vase and put Charles's bunch in instead. Mr Pinn looked hurt. Eclaire noticed, but her mother didn't. Eclaire quickly picked up her dad's bunch of flowers and stuffed them in a milk bottle full of water and put them on the table too, which meant none of the diners could see each other over the flowers. Charles noticed this and gave Eclaire a big smile.

Oh dear, he's nice, she thought. Should I try to wreck his wedding?

But she had gone too far to turn back now. The thought of the Fab Four and the Puke-Pink-Dress-of-Horrors spurred her on. She had failed to get Charles's jacket off, so she put Plan B into action.

"Oh, whooooopsy," said Eclaire, as she

accidentally-on-purpose knocked a glass full of wine in Charles's direction. "Oh, your *poor* jacket! I'm *so* sorry!"

"I see you're still the same as when your dance class was doing *The Story of Noah*," snorted Mary, "and the teacher said you might like to audition for the part of the Ark."

"Oh, a speck of wine won't harm," said Charles, kindly. But Eclaire had virtually ripped the jacket from him and was making off with it in the direction of the sink.

"No no, we must sponge it," she said, "might stain." She hastily shoved the letters in the pocket alongside his handkerchief – and felt an enormous sense of relief. She returned the jacket to Charles. Part one of the plan was accomplished. Now she had to find a way of getting Mary to discover the letters...

As Eclaire was pondering this, and as Mrs Pinn was serving watercress soup with little crusty bits in it that she called '*croutons*' but were actually bits of old dry bread, the phone rang. Eclaire made a violent grab for it.

"'Allo, 'allo, may I speak wiz Sharrrrles?" It was Owl, of course, with an extremely strange accent.

"Speak *up!*" said Eclaire (they had all forgotten Owl's tiny shy voice, when concocting their plan), and then she turned to the others. "It's not a very good line, but I think it's for you, Mary."

"How odd. Must be Mum," Mary picked up the receiver.

"'Allo, 'allo, Sharrrrles?"

"No, this is Mary. Who do you want? Charles?"

Click, *whirrrrr*. Owl put down the phone.

"It's gone dead," said Mary, hanging up. "Sounded like a French woman. I *thought* she was asking for Charles. Must've been a wrong number."

Five minutes later, just as everyone was wondering what to do with their soup, which was inedible, the phone rang again.

Eclaire grabbed it.

"'Allo. Please, may I speak with Sharrrles. Tell heeeem is Rose."

"It's her again," said Eclaire, innocently. "She says she's called Rose. Seems to want you, Charles."

"Must be a work thing," said Charles. "Sorry, Mrs Pinn – I gave them this number in case anything came up." He took the phone from Eclaire.

"Hello, Charles here. Who is this?"

61

"Sharrrrrles darleeeeng!" shouted Owl at the top of her voice, hoping everyone round the table would hear. "Sharrrrles! We must meet sooner than we arranged! Darth eees suspicious."

"Who is this?" asked Charles, looking puzzled.

"Oooo do you theenk? It is I, Rose! Ooooo else?" Owl was now giving full rein to her ambition to act. And, as is often the case when people are speaking in public, her stutter had vanished completely!

"Sorry. You must have the wrong number."

"Don't do thees to me, Sharrrrles. I yam dyeeeeng for yourrr lerve!"

But Charles had put the phone down.

"Strange woman," he shrugged. "Sounded drunk."

Mrs Pinn took this opportunity to remove the full plates of soup and to start carving the chicken.

"No potatoes for you dear," Mrs Pinn said, as Eclaire reached for the roast potatoes. "No gravy, dear, it's thickened," she said, as Eclaire reached for the gravy. "No, not those, they're buttered, these veg are for you," she added, handing Eclaire some stringy beans.

String? Or beans?

"Oh, you're much too young to diet, aren't you?" Charles remarked.

Eclaire was beginning to like him more and more. In fact, she was starting to see it as her mission to rescue him from the clutches of Mary.

"Too young to diet, perhaps, but hardly too small, eh, Claire? Do your friends still call you Eclaire? Or just Fattypuff?" chortled skinny Mary, piling gravy and potatoes and buttered vegetables on to her own plate. Eclaire regretted the Fab Four's decision not to try poison.

Brrrr! Brrrr! Brrrr!

This time Mrs Pinn picked it up.

"'Allo, must speak wiz Shaaaarrles. Eeees urgent."

"I'm afraid you have the wrong number," said Mrs Pinn, frostily.

"No, no, no-o-o-o-o," croaked Owl, desperately (it was hard keeping up the fake French accent). "Shaaaarles Smeeeth! I lerve eeem. I lerrrve eeeem weeeth orl my 'art!"

"Well, there is a Charles Smith here..." said Mrs Pinn, confused now.

Charles took the phone again.

"Shaaarrrrles, Sharles, I lerve yoooo. You must come to me now!"

"I'm afraid you have the wrong Charles Smith," said Charles calmly, putting down the receiver.

"How hilarious," giggled Mary. "Some mad Frenchwoman with a wrong number in love with another Charles Smith!"

"Well, there must be thousands of them," said Charles, sitting down again.

"Yes, darling, and I'm still marrying you, despite your boring name!" And Mary blew him a very soppy kiss, which made Eclaire furious. What was she to do now? She had to get Mary to read the letters, otherwise the whole plot would go up in smoke. And she doubted whether Owl would have the courage to phone a fifth time. Suddenly, inspiration struck.

She grabbed the gravy, spilling a lake of it over her top.

"Our nimble-fingered friend strikes again," said Mary, jumping up so the gravy would not ooze on to her expensive little dress.

"Quick! Your hanky!" blurted Eclaire to Charles.

To her delight, he pulled out the hanky and with

64

it came the two letters, one still smelling very strongly of perfume (Flash must have emptied the whole bottle on to it). The letters, delightfully, fell on top of Eclaire's plate as Charles bent over her. She brushed them off in Mary's direction and Mary could not help catching a glimpse of a few words: "Good heavens darling, 'powerful lips' – what on earth's this?" she asked.

And then, to Eclaire's mounting excitement, Mary read the pink letter.

"It seems to be from, er Rose. To you. *What* a passionate girl," said Mary in a chilly voice, quickly unfolding the blue letter. A silence had descended on the table.

"And this one's from you to her," Mary's voice was freezing by now. The atmosphere in the Pinn's dining room was like the North Pole. Mary read on and Eclaire felt herself go redder and redder until she thought she would burst. Soon the happy couple would split up. The wedding would be off. She would be *freeeee*. And so would Charles. But to Eclaire's horror, Mary started to titter, then to giggle, then to roar with laughter.

"Oh Charles, this is a hoot! Listen! 'Awash with passion...your beautiful ecstatically lovely eyes... I long for the thrill of your hot bosom...' Oh, no, really, it's too much. As if you would ever write such rubbish!" and Mary nearly exploded with laughter.

Charles took the letters and soon he was laughing his head off, too. "Don't know how you could have taken this one seriously, even for a second!" he said, nearly hysterical, waving the pink one in the air. "'Torrid longing...your manly form...powerful lips...' What a brilliant joke. It must be someone from the office. Maybe Philip? Or Sylvie, perhaps?"

He waved both letters around and Mr and Mrs Pinn guffawed along with him. This was just the kind of joke people did play on young couples, ho ho ho.

Brrrr! Brrrr! Brrrr!

"Oh, please don't let it be Owl having a final try," prayed Eclaire silently, reaching for the phone.

But Charles had got there first.

"'Aaaalloo, 'allo, Sharrrrrles!"

"Rose, my darling. We mustn't speak. I had to pretend not to know you last time. Mary was in the room. Hush! She's coming back." Then Charles whispered into the phone, "I'll see you tomorrow, at the harbour, as arranged."

Eclaire's heart was in her mouth. What could poor Owl be thinking? That the trick had worked only too well? That Charles really did have a secret love called Rose? Help.

"But...er...Sharrrrrles...errr...mph. I-I can't."

"Oh, don't worry," laughed Charles, "we know it's a joke."

Silence.

"We've rumbled you," continued Charles into the phone. "Jolly good one though."

"Did Eclaire tell you?" gasped Owl.

Since everyone had gone very quiet, in order to listen to this vital call, they all heard what Owl said.

Charles put the phone down and turned to look at Eclaire.

Everyone else at the table turned to look at Eclaire, too.

Eclaire knew that she was now such a bright scarlet that she had every chance of escaping detection and being mistaken for a vast tomato. She also felt so hot that she hoped she might just melt and ooze, like tomato sauce, under the door, before anyone could grab her. But, like a tomato, she was rooted to the spot. The seconds seemed to crawl by more slowly than centuries. The clock tick-tocked in the stifling silence. Eight eyes, stretched round with amazement, drilled holes into Eclaire's soul.

And then the silence was broken.

"Claire! Brilliant! I didn't know you had it in you!"

screamed Mary, throwing her arms round her.

"Yes. Jolly good. Jolly funny," agreed Charles.

Mr and Mrs Pinn looked relieved at the happy couple's response.

"Still, really, *'hot bosom'*, Claire. Well, well."

"That's just the sort of joke I'd have loved to play at your age. On silly old romantic soppy couples like us," tittered Mary.

"She's not so bad after all," realised Eclaire, with an enormous feeling of relief. But even though no one had shouted at her, even though she seemed to have escaped...her joy was tinged with gloom.

She had to face the facts. The happy couple had not stormed out of the house vowing never to speak to each other again. They had not even had the mildest of lovers' tiffs. Instead, they had simply proved that they shared the same sense of humour. They were made for each other. The wedding would obviously go ahead. Twigs and Jumbos started tomorrow at 11.30. Now, she was doomed to go.

Six

Brrr! Brrr! Brrr!

This time, the phone was ringing in Lizzy's house, next door to Eclaire's. It was 7.10 on Saturday morning, the night after the disastrous dinner party.

Upstairs, Lizzy and Owl were sleeping like logs, having stayed up half the night talking about the total failure of their plan. Owl had stayed with Lizzy – she had been far too upset to go home.

Brrr! Brrr! Brrr!

Who can that be? thought Lizzy, as she rolled over, hugged the duvet and a clammy hot water bottle, and went straight back to sleep.

But Owl, who was a lighter sleeper, sprang up from her sleeping-bag feeling nervous. Her fears were confirmed when Lizzy's mum banged on the door.

"Lizzy, Em!" shouted Mrs Wigan, "is Claire in there with you?"

Lizzy rolled over. "Hrmmmphh," she snored.

Owl shook her furiously. "Wake up, Lizzy! No! She's not here!" she shouted over her shoulder.

A frantic-looking Mrs Wigan hurtled into the room and started searching behind the curtains, under very small cushions, scattered books and mounds of festering socks, that were all quite obviously not large enough to shelter Eclaire.

"What's happening?" mumbled Lizzy.

"This is serious, girls," said Mrs Wigan. "Please own up if Claire stayed the night. I won't be cross. Please. Where is she?"

"Sh-she's n-not h-here, honestly," stuttered Owl.

Lizzy was now awake, sensing the urgency in the air.

"What's happened, what do you mean?" she asked, groggily.

"Claire's gone missing. Her mother just phoned. She can't find her anywhere," said Mrs Wigan, looking desperate.

"She's probably still asleep," said Lizzy. "It's only 7:15 and this is Saturday!"

"Lizzy, don't be silly," Mrs Wigan gave her daughter one of her looks. Mrs Wigan's looks could freeze you in your tracks. They were one of the reasons Lizzy had always hated her frizzy hair, it reminded her of snakes. She worried that if she started getting that same look in her eyes, she might turn into a gorgon who killed you with a glance.

"Don't you think her mother would have looked for her in bed, for goodness sake? That's exactly what worried her. She thought she heard some odd noises for so early in the morning and she went to check if Claire was all right and...she found...a pillow in the bed! It looks as if Claire's run away," Mrs Wigan said, in a very trembly voice. She was near to tears. And, quite suddenly, so were Owl and Lizzy.

Surely Eclaire could not have run away? Not sensible, funny, comforting Eclaire.

"I'll have to tell her Claire's not here – and phone the police."

"No! She must have gone to Flash's house!" yelled Lizzy suddenly. That *must* be it, surely. Poor old Eclaire must have woken up early. She must have felt really fed up with herself and Owl for blowing the plan, and gone to cry on Flash's shoulder.

"Of course," said Mrs Wigan, sighing with relief.

Lizzy dialled Flash immediately.

But Eclaire wasn't there. Flash said she'd cycle round straight away.

"Where else could she possibly be?" Mrs Wigan was crying, now.

Together, the girls phoned round other friends, but no one had seen Eclaire.

By now, Flash had arrived on her rusty old bike, still coughing and spluttering as she fought off the lurgi. "This is a disaster...I can't believe Eclaire would do this. She can't be that upset about the wedding."

"No, but she's *really* upset about Twigs and Jumbos," said Lizzy.

"What was that Lizzy?" Mrs Wigan heard them talking.

"W-we have to tell her," whispered Owl. "W-we have to tell her ab-about the dress – and-and everything. W-we owe it t-to Eclaire."

They poured the whole sorry story out to Lizzy's

mother, explaining the forged letters, phone calls and everything.

"Oh dear. Oh dear. I'll go next door," said Mrs Wigan, hurrying away to find Eclaire's mother, with the three girls trailing behind her.

"Oh no," sighed Eclaire' mum. "So you weren't playing a joke on Charles and Mary after all?"

Lizzy, Owl and Flash shook their heads and looked at their feet.

"You were deadly serious? You know, this is exactly the sort of thing you read about in the papers. Horrible mothers nagg their children and then children run away. And now I've done it to my own dear Claire. I had no idea she minded so much. How could I have been so stupid?"

"Excuse m-me," whispered Owl in her ear. "C-could I p-possibly s-see the b-bridesmaid's dress?"

"Oh, it's horrible, you don't want to see it. It's..." and Lizzy slapped her hand over her mouth. She had nearly broken her vow to Eclaire.

"But why?" asked Mrs Pinn.

"J-just m-might give us a c-clue," said Owl, mysteriously.

But the dress had gone!

"It's vanished!" said Mrs Pinn.

"W-where d-did it come from?" Owl asked innocently.

"*True-sew Bridal Wear*, in town, but why in the world should that matter now?" snapped Eclaire's mother. "I want my daughter, not the silly dress!"

Everyone agreed, feeling rather irritated with Owl's tactless questions. Lizzy's imagination had begun to run riot. Suppose she were never to see her lovely friend, her *best* friend in the world, ever again? Suppose, suppose...the very *worst* had already happened and Eclaire was lying in a ditch somewhere? Lizzy was now sobbing frantically. Flash, holding back her own tears, was trying to be practical, the adults were talking feverishly.

And in the general chaos that followed, with everybody panicking, crying, ringing relatives, neighbours, police, Owl slipped out.

Owl had an idea. She also had just enough money to pay for a bus fare into town. There was a woman at the bus stop who gave her a very peculiar look. Owl was used to people giving her funny looks because she was so small. She knew what the woman was bound to be thinking:

"Why is that little girl waiting for a bus on her own? She looks about seven. Perhaps I'd better ask her if she's all right."

'P-please d-don't ask,' Owl prayed to herself. She got very embarrassed by people drawing attention to her, which is why she had never dared to admit to anyone except the Fab Four that she wanted to be an actress. The woman edged a little nearer to her and Owl thought of making a run for it, but luckily the bus swept into sight just at that moment. The woman started fussing with her shopping bags and Owl hopped on the bus and ran upstairs. The next twenty minutes were very hard for Owl. She was as worried as anyone about

Eclaire's diasappearance and hoped against hope that her idea was right. But perhaps she was on a wild goose chase? She didn't dare let herself think about it.

She arrived at *True-sew Bridal Wear* at 8:40, just in time to see Eclaire emerge. Owl felt a huge rush of relief. She had kept her emotions under control quite well until now, but seeing Eclaire bouncing out of the shop made her realise just how worried she had been and how important her friends were to her.

"Owl! How did you know I was here? Is that your dressing-gown you're wearing?" said Eclaire, looking Owl up and down.

To her horror, Owl realised she was still wearing her dressing-gown and a pair of silk slippers. No wonder that woman at the bus stop had given her such a funny look – especially since the Molly Mouse pyjama top she'd had for four years was clearly visible.

She hated being so tiny. It was hard to persuade her mother to buy her new stuff when she never grew out of anything...

"W-why d-didn't you t-tell everyone where you were g-going? You scared the life out of us all!" said Owl.

"What's all the fuss about?" said Eclaire cheerily.

"Everyone thought you'd run away!" wailed Owl.

"No! Did they? Were they upset?" said Eclaire, with a mixture of surprise and pleasure. "I was going straight back. My family don't usually come looking for me before 9:30 on a Saturday and anyway, I put a pillow in my bed to look like I was asleep..."

"That's the kind of idea th-that w-works in d-detective stories," said Owl. "R-real m-mothers know the difference between a p-pillow and a daughter."

"My mother doesn't," muttered Eclaire.

"Oh c-come on, Eclaire, that's not fair."

"Oh, isn't it?" snapped Eclaire and then looked guilty. "I am sorry everyone was worried. But really, am I the type of person who'd just up and run away from something? I thought I'd just slip back in quietly. And I knew the *True-sew* shop was open early on Saturday for mad brides with last-minute dress panics."

Then Eclaire gestured to the large box she was carrying. "You know what's in here, don't you, Owl?" she said.

"I-I th-think so," murmured Owl.

Eclaire let her have a peek. "Don't tell, let me show them," she said as they ran for the bus. "Did you tell my mum everything? I mean, about me being scared about Twigs and Jumbos and all that?"

"S-scared?" asked Owl timidly. "I th-thought you w-were m-more cross?"

"Well, I was cross. But I was scared, too. I was scared I'd be the fattest there...and that everyone would laugh. I was scared they'd give me a horrible exercise programme with handstands and stuff that I just can't do. Most of all, I was scared at the thought of not seeing a choc bar for a whole week! I hope she won't still make me go – after she's seen this."

"Oh, h-help," blurted Owl. "We should have

rung her up! She'll have helicopters looking for you soon."

But by now they were on the bus, which travelled only slightly faster through the heavy traffic than a very tired snail.

When Owl and Eclaire finally arrived home there were no helicopters, just two police officers taking a statement. They both smiled knowingly when Eclaire fell into her mother's arms.

There was much hugging and kissing and saying 'sorry' and then Eclaire said, "Wait a minute, I've got something to show you all."

She disappeared, clutching the *True-sew* box.

Surely she's not going to try on the Puke-Pink-Dress-of-Horrors is she? thought Lizzy.

Four minutes later, a vision of loveliness appeared at the top of the Pinn's stairs.

It was Eclaire. She was wearing a sunshine-yellow, extra-large, smooth, elegant, magnificent, beautiful dress. It fitted her perfectly. She fitted it perfectly. She and the dress slid down the banisters together and arrived, unruffled (there was not, Lizzy was happy to see, a single frill, flounce, ruffle or net to be seen), at the foot of the stairs.

"Claire. You look magnificent," said her mother.

Which is what everyone agreed she did look, and everyone agreed she was.

In the sunshine-yellow dress, Eclaire even quite enjoyed the wedding, mainly because the happy couple had thoughtfully laid on a vast supply of meringues. And Twigs and Jumbos was never mentioned in the Pinn household ever again, well hardly ever.

Read more about

Frizzy Lizzy, Flash,
Eclaire and Owl

in the other FAB FOUR books.

The
Love
Bug

Ros Asquith

One

"Oh, I wish you could understand how much I love you," Flash blinked back a tear as she hugged her favourite pony. Flame was a chestnut gelding, just 12 hands high, with a roman nose, stubby legs and a very shaggy mane indeed. He looked more like a baby guinea pig than a pony and more like a cuddly toy than either. Flame was due to be retired from the riding stables that month and Flash was sure he would go to the knacker's to be made into pet food. Flash had asked if she could look after Flame but the riding instructor just laughed like a drain and said, "In a council flat?" He added it was nothing to do with him – it was up to the owner who was never there. Flash had worked every spare hour at the stables to earn money to save Flame. She had worked out exactly what to do. She already had £60 and was planning to ask the stable owner about it that Sunday.

But she hadn't told anyone yet, not even the Fab Four.

"I love you so, so much," she continued, stroking Flame's funny little crooked white blaze, "but no one wants you any more, you're too old, you're just too old."

"I'm not that old," said a cheery voice in her ear.

Flash squeaked. Her dream had come true! Flame could talk!

"Not that much older than you, I should think," the voice went on.

Flash blushed scarlet. It was hard to say which was redder, her face, her hair, or Flame's forelock. The voice, naturally, was not a pony's voice. Even if ponies could speak (and Flash was sure that with the right training and a lot of kindness they could) they would be likely to have a sort of whinnying, snuffling tone. This voice was certainly a boy's voice. A rather soft, American drawl. And there was only one voice that Flash knew that sounded anything like that, and that was Tom's.

Tom was the gorgeous new stable boy who everyone fancied and Flash, though she didn't like to admit it, could see why. She could see why especially at this moment, as she turned, her face the colour of a London bus, to look at him. He had blond hair and the kind of California surfer's tan that you don't get on a wet English October afternoon. His green eyes twinkled mischievously at Flash as she turned to face him.

"I m-meant Flame was old," stammered Flash, thinking that if the ground opened now and she disappeared forever it might be worth it, just to have bathed in that smile.

"That's all right then," gleamed Tom. "You coming up tomorrow?"

"Oh...yeah," said Flash trying to be casual. She nonchalantly patted Flame's neck. Then she rather less nonchalantly disentangled her watch strap from his mane before sauntering out of the yard and tripping gracefully over a bucket.

"Whoopsy," said Tom, helping her up with a strong arm and beaming another rocket powered grin that made Flash dizzy.

She was late for a meeting of the Fab Four and rang them to suggest they start without her. She was definitely feeling a teensy bit, well, wobbly.

To find out what happens next...
Read the rest of

The Love Bug

Bad Hair Day

Frizzy Lizzy has tried everything ever invented
to tame her wild hair. Can her brother's
chemistry set succeed where all else has failed?
When you're as desperate as Lizzy, anything's
worth a go...

1-84121-476-0

Drama Queen

Owl's so shy she's never taken part in anything involving more than two people – even a conversation. But Owl's got big dreams and nothing's going to stop her being in the school play. Will she get the starring role or should she play something a little quieter, a piece of scenery perhaps?

Three's a Crowd

The Fab Four are off on a school trip.
But can Owl cope with taking part in scary
activities like abseiling, white-water canoeing
and worst of all, sharing a cabin with bully
bossy-boots, Bernice Berens? She'll have the
Fab Four to help, of course!

More Orchard Red Apples

☐ **Bad Hair Day**	Ros Asquith	1 84121 480 9	**£3.99**
☐ **Frock Shock**	Ros Asquith	1 84121 482 5	**£3.99**
☐ **The Love Bug**	Ros Asquith	1 84121 478 7	**£3.99**
☐ **Drama Queen**	Ros Asquith	1 84121 476 0	**£3.99**
☐ **All for One**	Ros Asquith	1 84121 362 4	**£3.99**
☐ **Three's a Crowd**	Ros Asquith	1 84121 360 8	**£3.99**
☐ **Pink Knickers Aren't Cool**	Jean Ure	1 84121 835 9	**£3.99**
☐ **Girls Stick Together**	Jean Ure	1 84121 839 1	**£3.99**
☐ **Girls Are Groovy**	Jean Ure	1 84121 843 x	**£3.99**
☐ **Boys Are OK!**	Jean Ure	1 84121 847 2	**£3.99**
☐ **Do Not Read This Book**	Pat Moon	1 84121 435 3	**£4.99**

Orchard Red Apples are available from all good bookshops,
or can be ordered direct from the publisher:
Orchard Books, PO BOX 29, Douglas IM99 1BQ
Credit card orders please telephone 01624 836000 or fax 01624 837033
or visit our Internet site: www.wattspub.co.uk
or e-mail: bookshop@enterprise.net for details.

To order please quote title, author and ISBN
and your full name and address.
Cheques and postal orders should be made payable to 'Bookpost plc.'
Postage and packing is FREE within the UK
(overseas customers should add £1.00 per book).
Prices and availability are subject to change.